THIS BOOK IS NOT A PIECE OF CHEESE!

by Benjamin Bird

PICTURE WINDOW BOOKS
capstonepub.com

THIS BOOK IS NOT A PIECE OF CHEESE!
is published by Picture Window Books,
A Capstone Imprint
1710 Roe Crest Drive
North Mankato, Minnesota 56003
www.capstonepub.com

CAPS32490

Cataloging-in-Publication Data is available
on the Library of Congress website.
ISBN: 978-1-62370-128-4 (paper over board)
ISBN: 978-1-4795-5231-3 (library hardcover)
ISBN: 978-1-4795-6163-6 (eBook)

DESIGNED BY:
Russell Griesmer

ILLUSTRATED BY:
Comicup Studio
Carmen Pérez — Pencils
Francesc Figueres Farrès — Inks
Gloria Caballe — Color

Printed in the United States of America in North Mankato, Minnesota.
052014   008087CGF14